The Boxcar Children Mysteries

THE MYSTERY OF THE MISSING POP IDOL

created by
GERTRUDE CHANDLER WARNER

Albert Whitman & Company
Chicago, Illinois

Library of Congress Cataloging-in-Publication Data

Warner, Gertrude Chandler.
The mystery of the missing pop idol / created by Gertrude Chandler Warner ;
interior illustrations by Anthony VanArsdale.
pages cm—(The Boxcar children mysteries ; 138)
Summary: "During auditions for the show *Pop Star Sensation* at the local mall,
one of the judges, a famous pop star, disappears, and the Aldens must find out
where she went"—Provided by publisher.
[1. Mystery and detective stories. 2. Missing persons—Fiction.
3. Singers—Fiction. 4. Brothers and sisters—Fiction.
5. Orphans—Fiction.] I. VanArsdale, Anthony, illustrator. II. Title.
PZ7.W244Mtn 2015
[Fic]—dc23
2014027701

Printed in the United States of America
10 9 8 7 6 5 4 3 2 1 LB 20 19 18 17 16 15 14

Cover art by Logan Kline
Interior illustrations by Anthony VanArsdale

For more information about Albert Whitman & Company,
visit our web site at www.albertwhitman.com.

Contents

THE MYSTERY OF THE MISSING POP IDOL

CHAPTER 1

A Pop Star Arrives

Be the next big pop star! Audition for Pop Star Sensation *today!* read the giant sign hanging over the entrance to Silver City Mall.

"Are you ready to sing, Violet?" asked twelve-year-old Jessie Alden.

Violet Alden, dressed in her best purple skirt, blushed and hid behind the oldest Alden child, fourteen-year-old Henry. "You're making me nervous," she said shyly.

"Go, Violet!" cheered her younger brother, Benny, who was six. "You can do it!"

Violet's favorite TV show, *Pop Star Sensation*, was holding tryouts in Silver City that day. The show's judges were looking for talented singers who might become the next big music star. Contestants had to be at least Henry's age to compete, so Violet was too young, but she was hoping for the chance to sing on the show, even if it would only be for fun.

Violet and her three siblings were going behind the scenes of *Pop Star Sensation* for the day. Their grandfather had an old friend who was the producer of the show, and he had invited the children to watch the filming. All four of the children were excited, especially Violet, who never missed an episode and sang along to every song.

At ten, Violet was the youngest Alden sister and the shyest of the four children. Although she was bashful—especially in situations like this—Violet was a very talented musician. She played violin, and her ear for music helped her sing very well. Even if Violet was quiet around other people, her siblings had listened to her sing for years.

"Violet," said Benny, "you're the best singer I know. You shouldn't be nervous at all!"

"That's right, Violet," said Jessie. "You're going to do really well. And we'll be here for you."

The Alden children had always supported each other. When they had become orphans, they ran away and lived in an abandoned boxcar in the woods. They had been afraid to live with their grandfather, worrying that he would be a mean man. But when the children realized what a nice man Grandfather Alden was, they were happy to live with him in his big house. He was so nice, in fact, that he had the children's boxcar moved to the backyard for a playhouse.

"And if Grandfather finishes with his business in time," said Henry, "he'll be cheering for you too."

Grandfather had dropped them off at the mall earlier that morning. He had a business meeting to attend elsewhere in Silver City, but he planned to meet up with his grandchildren later that day.

The four Alden children turned and looked behind them. The mall's vast parking lot was filling up with thousands of other people. They had all dressed up to stand out, hoping to look funny or fancy or flashy so that they would get a chance to appear on the TV show. Near the Aldens was a woman with heavy makeup and a hot-pink feather boa wrapped around her neck. Behind her stood a man in a cowboy hat, cowboy boots, and leather cowboy chaps. He twirled a lasso while singing a country-western tune. Behind the cowboy was a family with more children than the Aldens.

"Look, guys," said Benny, pointing at the children, who were all dressed in matching gray outfits and green neckties. "There are seven brothers and sisters in that family!"

"It's not polite to point, Benny," said Jessie. But Jessie was very impressed by the beautiful voices she heard as the family of five sisters and two brothers practiced singing together. The Aldens listened until they became aware of another sound.

From the back of the crowd, a murmur had begun to grow louder. Soon the murmur became a roar of cheers. The Aldens turned to see what all the fuss was about. The crowd moved out of the way for a line of big black cars driving through the mall parking lot.

The cars had black-tinted windows so no one could see inside. The cars made their way to the front entrance, coming to a stop near where the Aldens stood.

"I wonder who's inside," Jessie said.

"I bet it's someone important," said Henry.

"Do you think it might be Madlynn Rose?" Violet asked, naming her favorite singer.

The answer to Violet's question came soon enough. The door to the first black car opened. As soon as the person inside climbed out, the crowd began to boo.

"Why is everyone booing?" Benny asked. "That's not very nice." Neither he nor his siblings booed since all four of them tried to be nice to everyone.

"It's Wilfred Mayflower," said Jessie. "He's *not* very nice."

Wilfred Mayflower was the head judge of *Pop Star Sensation*. He was a short, round man, and to the Alden children, he seemed even shorter and rounder in person. He wore

a spotless white suit and shining white shoes. He also had a very shiny bald head.

Wilfred Mayflower spent each episode of *Pop Star Sensation* hurting contestants' feelings. When many of the contestants finished singing a song, Wilfred would yell, "That was *horrible*!" He had a thick British accent that the Aldens thought made him sound smart and scary at the same time. Violet hoped Wilfred Mayflower would be nice if she ever got the chance to sing for him.

The crowd kept booing Wilfred Mayflower, but he didn't seem to mind. In fact, he seemed to enjoy it. He smiled as the boos grew louder and he waved to the mob of people who booed him. Wilfred reached the entrance to the Silver City Mall just as the door to the next black SUV opened.

"Is this going to be Madlynn Rose?" Violet asked.

"I bet it will be Esty Gadooj," said Henry.

Henry was right. Out of the second vehicle climbed a woman the children had seen on TV. Esty Gadooj was a famous singer and dancer. She was also famous for the crazy clothes she wore.

Jessie thought that Esty had dressed especially wild for the *Pop Star Sensation* auditions at the Silver City Mall. Her hair was dyed hot pink. Her clothes were puffy and the color of cotton candy—pastel pink and blue and yellow—with bright lights blinking all over the sleeves and legs. Flashy and flashing, Esty looked like a walking, talking neon sign.

"Why is everyone still booing?" Benny asked. "I thought people liked Esty Gadooj."

"They do," said Jessie. "They're just cheering 'Gadooooj!' and it sounds like they're booing."

Esty Gadooj strutted up to a microphone set up by the entrance to the mall. "Good morning, Silver City!" she said. "We are so excited to visit, darlings. We wish you all the best of luck today at the auditions. I'm sure you'll all be marvelous! Now, I'd like to introduce you to the third and final judge, who's much nicer than Mr. Mayflower—and much prettier too. My darlings, please say hello to Madlynn Rose!"

Now the crowd *really* began to cheer.

"Did you hear that?" Violet asked her siblings. "It's Madlynn Rose! It's really her!"

The door to the third and final black car opened and out climbed the young pop singer who was Violet's hero.

"She's wearing purple," said Violet, "just like me!"

Madlynn Rose was in a purple dress and purple shoes, and purple ribbons tied her dark-blond hair up into a tower atop her head. Violet knew the pop star wasn't much older than she was—she was just a couple years older than Henry.

"I can't believe it's her!" Violet said. "She's a real person."

When Madlynn Rose stepped up to the microphone and began to sing, Violet thought the pop star's voice sounded as amazing as it did on TV. Performing one of her latest hits, the pop star sang:

"It feels like time to say hello,
But, sorry, now I've got to go.
One last thing you've got to know,

This won't be good-bye, oh no.
This won't be good-bye.
This won't be good-bye."

Many people in the crowd were singing along. One of the loudest singers was Violet, who knew every word.

The pop star held the microphone out to the crowd to let them know she loved their singing as much as they loved hers. When she finished her song, she placed the microphone back on its stand, waved to her fans, and hurried into the Silver City Mall.

"You sounded amazing singing along with Madlynn Rose," Jessie told Violet.

"You sure did," said Henry.

"That was Madlynn Rose's new song," Violet said. "It's called 'This Won't Be Good-bye,' and it's the one I was hoping to sing in front of the judges...if I get the chance."

The black cars pulled away and the crowd waited for the mall doors to open.

"Is it just me," said Violet, "or have we been waiting a long time?"

"We have," said Jessie. "But we'll be inside soon enough. Just be patient."

Suddenly there was another roar from the crowd.

"Look! The door is opening!" shouted one of the kids in the singing group family. "I bet it's Madlynn Rose!"

"Or maybe it's Esty Gadooj!" shouted the cowboy.

"I can't see anything!" shouted the woman with the pink feather boa. "But I sure hope it's that cute, little Wilfred Mayflower!"

The thousands of people in the crowd edged closer to the mall's front doors.

The Aldens looked at the doors hopefully. "Are they going to let us in?" Benny asked.

"I don't know," said Henry, "but I see someone."

"Who is it?" Violet asked.

Someone stepped out of the mall. The crowd—and the Aldens—tried to see who it could be. Everyone pushed and murmured with excitement.

CHAPTER 2

A Pop Star Disappears

The person who stepped outside wasn't Madlynn Rose or Esty Gadooj. It wasn't even Wilfred Mayflower. It was a serious-looking man in a black suit and black sunglasses. He seemed mysterious.

The crowd was pushing to get closer to the doors.

"I sure hope they let us inside soon," Jessie said. "That man's giving me the creeps!"

"Yeah," said Benny. "He's even scarier than Wilfred Mayflower."

"Let's just be patient," said Henry, "I'm sure today's action will begin sooner than any of us realize."

Like the rest of the crowd, the Aldens settled down to wait again. They waited and waited, but the doors to the mall didn't open.

"I'm getting tired," said Benny, "and hungry too."

"You're always hungry, Benny," Jessie said.

"The longer we wait, the more nervous I get," said Violet. "I really want to get inside and sing."

"Me too," said a voice from behind the Aldens.

In all of the excitement, the crowd had shifted. The woman with the pink boa, the cowboy, and the family in matching outfits were no longer nearby. Now there was a girl in line behind them a few years older than Henry.

She had long blond hair with a flower in it and wore sunglasses with lenses shaped like flowers. She had on jeans and a denim jacket, both of which were covered with flower patches. In one hand, she carried a guitar case that was covered with colorful flower stickers that looked shiny and new.

"Cool guitar case," said Benny. "What do those words say?"

"Lonny," said the girl, pointing to the letters stuck to one side of the case. "That's my name. The other side says, 'Dreams.' That's me. Lonny Dreams."

"Lonny Dreams, huh?" said Henry. "That's a different name. Pretty cool."

"Are you here to sing for *Pop Star Sensation*, Lonny?" asked Violet.

"Yes, I am," said the girl. "How about you?"

"We're here to watch the show," said Jessie. "But our sister is going to sing a song by Madlynn Rose."

"Madlynn Rose doesn't write the songs she sings," said Lonny. "She sings songs written for her by other people. I write my own songs. I'm going to sing one of them for the judges."

"Well, I'm sure your song will sound really good," said Violet. "Will you play it for us?"

"I guess so," said Lonny. She set her flower-covered case on the ground and was taking out her guitar when the crowd began to cheer again.

"Are they cheering for Lonny?" asked Benny.

"No," said Henry. "They're cheering because the doors are opening again."

An older man with a headset and clipboard stepped outside the doors and walked up to the crowd. On his polo shirt was the logo for *Pop Star Sensation.*

"Pick us! Pick us!" shouted a group of voices from somewhere farther back in the crowd.

"Yee-haw!" shouted another voice behind the Aldens. "I'm gonna be on TV!"

"I want to meet that adorable Wilfred Mayflower!" a woman's voice shouted.

The whole crowd seemed to be trying to get the man's attention—except for Lonny Dreams, who hid behind her guitar. But the man headed straight for Henry, Jessie, Violet, and Benny Alden, barely noticing anyone else.

"Are you the Aldens?" the man asked.

"Yes, we are," said Henry.

"My name is Lester Freeman. I'm your

grandfather's friend," the man said. He looked as old as their grandfather, with a tan and wrinkled face, but his hair was longer and curlier and dyed a bright blond.

"Are you going to let us in?" asked Benny. "Finally?"

"That's not very polite," Jessie said to her little brother. Then she turned to Lester Freeman. "Thank you so much for inviting us."

"We're really excited to watch," said Violet, "and sing."

"You must be Violet Alden," Lester said. "You're even prettier than the pictures your grandfather has showed me. Okay, children, we have to start filming the show, so we'd better hurry. Follow me inside."

The doors of the mall closed behind the producer and the children, leaving everyone else to wait outside.

The Aldens had been to the Silver City Mall many times before and knew their way around.

"There's the movie theater!" said Benny, pointing to a poster with a Tyrannosaurus

Rex on it. "I want to see that new movie about dinosaurs!"

"Maybe Grandfather will take us later today," said Henry.

Lester led the children through the mall, down a long hallway, and into a large, busy studio filled with lights and cameras.

"This is where we're filming today's auditions," said Lester.

A crew of men and women wearing the same *Pop Star Sensation* shirts as Lester hurried around the room, plugging in cords and wires, looking into monitors, and arranging furniture. Lester pulled a couple of the workers aside and told them, "I'm hoping today's show will be a ratings bonanza!"

"A reading banana?" Benny asked Henry. "I didn't know bananas could read!"

"He said 'bonanza,'" Henry laughed. "A ratings bonanza. Ratings tell producers how many people watch a TV show. And a bonanza is something big or great. So he's hoping that lots of people will watch today's episode of *Pop Star Sensation* when it's on TV."

The Aldens looked past all the busy people and recognized the set from *Pop Star Sensation*.

On the back wall was the *Pop Star Sensation* logo. The lights and cameras all pointed to the long table that the Alden children knew from the TV show.

"Look!" Violet said. "It's the judges' table!"

Sitting behind the table were two of the show's famous judges—Wilfred Mayflower and Esty Gadooj.

"Those lights are really bright," Benny said. "And they're pretty warm too."

Wilfred Mayflower pulled a handkerchief from his pocket and wiped his shiny head and his wet face. "The heat is horrible!" he said. "Can we hurry this up, please? I haven't got all day."

"Yes, you do, darling," said Esty Gadooj. "Did you see how many people were outside? We'll be here until tomorrow if all of them are going to sing."

A third chair sat empty.

But before Violet could ask where her idol Madlynn Rose was, Lester spoke up. "That is why we need to get started," he said, talking

into his headset. "Please have the crowd start making its way into the mall. Single-file, please. We'll be ready to start the auditions shortly."

Then Lester turned to the Aldens. "We always film a practice take before we begin recording the actual show. This is to make sure the cameras are all working and the microphones sound right," he said. "Violet, would you like to be the singer for the practice take? It will be just like performing on *Pop Star Sensation*."

Violet was almost too excited to say anything, but she remembered her manners. "Thank you, Mr. Freeman. I would love to sing on the show."

Leaving Violet by the judges' table, the producer showed Henry, Jessie, and Benny to a row of chairs next to one of the cameras.

A woman with a dark suntan and lots of makeup sat in a chair next to them. She was tapping away on a tablet and talking on a cell phone, paying little attention to anything else that was going on.

"You'll be able to watch from here," Lester

told them. "Just be sure not to talk while we are filming."

"This is really cool," said Henry. "I've always wanted to learn how a real TV show is made."

"And Violet's always wanted to be on a real TV show," said Benny. "Just like Madlynn Rose."

"Are you fans of Madlynn Rose?" asked the woman sitting next to the children without looking up from her tablet or taking the phone from her ear.

"Our sister Violet is her biggest fan!" said Jessie.

"She's going to be singing in just a minute," said Benny. "Are you a fan of Madlynn Rose, too?"

"You could say that," said the woman. "I'm her mother."

"You must be really proud of your daughter," said Jessie.

"Well," said Madlynn Rose's mother, "I just wish she would work a little harder and do what I say. She's a pop star now, and she has to do interviews and perform at concerts.

She just wants to live the life of a regular teenager, but she needs to realize that she's *not* regular. She's famous, and she needs to start doing things to become more famous and to get more attention. How will I pay for my next vacation if she doesn't do enough to stay famous?"

"Being famous doesn't sound like much fun at all," Benny whispered to Jessie and Henry.

"Quiet on the set!" a voice yelled. It was Lester. The show was about to start.

Lester directed Violet to a microphone stand placed in front of the judges' table.

"Okay, Violet," the producer said, "you'll sing into this microphone."

Violet stepped up to the microphone and tapped it nervously. Then she looked at the judges. Wilfred Mayflower had his arms folded and looked very grumpy. Esty Gadooj smiled and sat waiting for Violet to begin. But the third chair at the judges' table was still empty.

"Is Madlynn Rose going to hear me sing?" Violet asked into the microphone. She pointed to the empty chair. The other two judges turned and looked at the chair in surprise.

"She was just here," said Esty Gadooj. "She must have gone to her dressing room to freshen up."

"How unprofessional!" exclaimed Wilfred Mayflower. "Like I said, I haven't got all day for this ridiculous behavior. I've been saying for some time that she has no place on this show, and that we have to get rid of her."

Lester stepped up onto the stage. "Does anyone know where Madlynn Rose went?" he asked the crew. Then he repeated the question into his headset.

The Aldens looked around the set. Something was wrong. Henry saw the camera crew turn off their cameras. Jessie saw the makeup artists whisper to one another. Madlynn Rose's mother stood up, her eyes wide. She abruptly ended her phone call and hurried off across the set.

"What's going on?" Benny asked.

"I don't know," said Jessie.

"Everyone, listen," Lester called out. "We have a situation here. The mall will be locked down while the security guards do a search.

Nobody repeat a word of what is going on!" His voice was serious.

A crew member approached the Aldens.

"I'm sorry," she said, "but Mr. Freeman thinks it's best if you wait back in the mall for now. We'll let you know when you can come back."

As the children were led back out into the mall, they could see that the crowd of hopeful singers now waited in a long line that wrapped around the whole building.

The door to the set shut behind the children. Then Benny finally said what they all had been afraid to say out loud.

"Madlynn Rose is missing!"

CHAPTER 3

Good and Bad Voices

"Ssshhh!" Jessie hushed her little brother. "We aren't supposed to say anything."

"Jessie's right," said Henry. "We also don't want to cause a panic by letting the news slip that Madlynn Rose is missing."

"I'm sorry," Benny whispered. "I won't talk about Madlynn Rose going missing anymore."

"Stop talking about it, then," said Violet. "I'm really sad about it."

Everything had happened so quickly that

the others hadn't had a chance to think about how Violet felt. She had wanted to sing for Madlynn Rose!

Jessie gave Violet a hug, and so did Henry. But Benny was looking at something else.

"Look!" Benny yelled. "It's that creepy guy with the sunglasses!"

Benny pointed to the door to the set. Sure enough, there, right outside the studio, stood the man in dark sunglasses and a black suit, the same mysterious man the children had seen outside the mall earlier that morning.

Just as soon as they noticed him, he disappeared around a corner.

Just then, a voice behind them spoke up.

"Did I hear you say that Madlynn Rose is missing?" the voice asked.

The four children turned around. There, at the front of the audition line, stood a young woman wearing a Madlynn Rose T-shirt. She carried a tablet and her eyes were wide.

"Sssshhh!" Benny said to the young woman. "It's a secret. We're not supposed to talk about it."

"It's not a secret anymore," she replied,

tapping away furiously on her tablet, "because in just a second, the whole world is going to know!"

"What are you doing?" Jessie asked. "Are you putting the news of Madlynn Rose's disappearance on the Internet?"

"That's exactly what I'm doing," said the young woman. "*Madlynn Rose Online* is about to break the news."

"*Madlynn Rose Online*?" said Violet. "That's my favorite website! Are you the one who runs it?"

"I sure am," said the young woman. "My name's Sophia, or Super Fan Sophia as I'm known online. My website has all the latest and greatest information about Madlynn Rose—her favorite foods, her favorite color, what she wears to all the awards shows, the lyrics to all of her hit songs, *everything*. I'm the biggest Madlynn Rose fan on Earth."

"That's not true," said Benny. "My sister Violet's the biggest Madlynn Rose fan there is. She's even going to sing a Madlynn Rose song for the *Pop Star Sensation* TV show."

"I *was* going to," said Violet sadly. "But now

Madlynn Rose is missing, so who knows if I'll get the chance. What if the show doesn't happen? This is terrible!"

"It's not very terrible for me," said Super Fan Sophia. "If I'm the one who reports this news first, my website will get *millions* of visitors. I'll be more famous and popular than ever!"

"But there's not really any news to report yet," said Henry. "We don't know what happened to Madlynn Rose or where she went."

"That's right," said Jessie. "So there's nothing for you to say on your website. Nobody's supposed to say anything about it either. It's all still a mystery."

"A mystery!" said Benny. "That sounds exciting. We should try to solve it. We've solved lots of mysteries."

Sophia rolled her eyes. "You're just kids," she said. "How could you solve mysteries? It's not like you're detectives or anything."

"We're a good team," said Henry. "And we *have* figured out quite a few mysteries. I think Benny's idea sounds pretty good. I think we should try to solve this mystery of the missing pop star."

"We'd better solve it," said Violet, "to help Madlynn Rose."

"And to help Violet get another chance to sing for her," said Benny.

"Isn't she a little young to sing on *Pop Star Sensation*?" asked Sophia.

"Our grandfather is friends with the show's producer," Henry explained. "Violet isn't going to compete on the show, but she wants to sing for Madlynn Rose."

"Well, I'm going to win the competition," said Sophia. "I'm not only Madlynn Rose's biggest fan, but I can also sing just like her."

"Why wouldn't you just want to sing like yourself?" asked a voice from behind them.

"What?" asked Sophia, turning around. "Who said that?"

The Aldens turned too. They saw the girl they'd met outside the mall that morning with the flower in her long blond hair. She still wore her sunglasses, even though she was inside now.

"Why would you want to sing just like

Madlynn Rose?" Lonny Dreams asked Sophia. She was taking her guitar from her flower-covered case.

"I'll have you know, I can sing even *better* than Madlynn Rose," Sophia snapped. "In fact, maybe *I* should be the big pop star instead of her. Maybe it's a good thing she's missing. Because then the world will see how talented I am. You know, maybe I won't say anything about Madlynn Rose missing on my website. Maybe I'll wait and tell the world that there is a new pop star—Super Fan Sophia!"

With that, Sophia began to sing the same song Madlynn Rose had sung to the crowd earlier that morning.

"She doesn't sound anything like Madlynn Rose," Jessie whispered to her siblings. They all nodded.

"She sounds like Watch when he howls," Benny whispered back. Watch was the Alden children's dog and sometimes he would howl when he sensed danger.

"*This won't be good-bye, oh no,*" sang Sophia. "*This won't be good-bye.*"

"I *wish* she would say good-bye," Benny

whispered to Violet. He tried not to say it too loud so that he wouldn't hurt Sophia's feelings, even if her singing was hurting his ears.

But as Sophia kept singing, another voice drowned hers out. This voice was louder but also much better:

"Everybody telling me what to do,
Everyone telling me who I should be,
But I can't be you or you or you.

I'll follow my dreams and be me.
So let me be me.
Please let me be me."

The singer was Lonny, who was strumming her purple guitar. A small crowd had gathered to listen, and when she finished her song, everyone clapped and cheered. The Aldens did too.

"I've never heard that song before," said Henry.

"Me either," said Violet. "But it was really nice."

"It was great!" cheered Benny.

"It wasn't *that* great," said Sophia, who put her tablet into her bag and stomped away. "Like I said, the next news that *Madlynn Rose Online* posts will be that *I* am the next *Pop Star Sensation* superstar!"

"Don't listen to her," Jessie told Lonny. "She's probably just jealous that she can't sing as well as you."

"I don't know if *anyone* can sing as well as you," said Violet. "I wish I could sing like that. That was a really nice song too."

"I wrote it myself," said Lonny.

"You did?" asked Violet. "That's amazing!"

"Thank you," Lonny said, blushing as much as Violet often did. "I was hoping to sing one of the songs I've written for the *Pop Star Sensation* judges today. But I couldn't help overhear what you guys were just talking about. You said someone is missing? And that the show might not happen?"

"It's a secret," Benny whispered.

"It's not going to stay a secret if you keep telling everyone," said Jessie.

"That's okay," said Lonny. "Your secret's safe with me."

"Madlynn Rose is missing," Benny continued. "And now we're going to solve the mystery and find her."

"That sounds exciting," Lonny said. "Let me know if you need my help, okay?"

"We will," said Henry. "But we're just getting started—"

"Look!" Benny cut in. "It's the creepy man again!"

There, standing in the same corner the children had seen him a few minutes ago, was the mysterious black-suited man with the sunglasses.

"Come on," said Henry. "Let's follow him."

Just then the loudspeakers of the mall's PA system called out their names.

"Henry, Jessie, Violet, and Benny Alden, please report to the main entrance. Repeat, Alden children, please come to the main entrance of the mall."

CHAPTER 4

Nobody In, Nobody Out

"That's us!" shouted Benny. "Someone's calling our names!"

"It must be mall security," said Jessie.

"Or maybe the police," said Benny.

"Maybe they know something about Madlynn Rose," said Violet. "Maybe they found her!"

"Come on, guys!" Henry called, already heading back the way they'd come that morning. "It's this way to the front entrance."

The Alden children dashed back through

the mall, past the audition line that seemed to never end.

Violet paused to look at a display for a store that sold sunglasses of all types. A pretty flowered pair had caught her eye.

"Ooh!" said Violet. "I want to buy these sunglasses sometime. They're just like the ones that girl Lonny has."

She wished she could take a closer look, but the others didn't stop. Violet had to sprint to catch up as they ran to the front entrance.

At last the Aldens reached the main doors of the mall, where a familiar face stood on the other side of the glass.

"Grandfather!" Benny yelled, running toward the door.

But two large security guards blocked the Aldens' path. "I'm sorry, kids," said one of the guards. "I can't let him in, and I can't let you leave."

"But that's our grandfather," said Henry. "He's here to watch our sister perform on *Pop Star Sensation*."

"Nobody in," said the second guard, "and nobody out."

Grandfather Alden looked at the children and nodded. "I'm afraid he's right," he said through the slightly opened door. "The mall is locked. I just spoke with Lester on the phone, and he said there is a bit of a situation."

"Does he mean the situation with Madlynn Rose missing?" Violet asked.

"Ssshhh!" hushed the other security guard. "That's a secret."

"Or it would be," said the first guard, "if anybody was missing."

"Oh, I get it," said Jessie. "You're not supposed to talk about Madlynn Rose missing."

"Whoever might be missing," said the second guard, "it's a secret."

The first guard pretended to zip his lip and throw away an imaginary key. "We already have enough to do, anyway, what with a shoplifter on the loose, swiping things from stores in the mall."

"But why can't Grandfather come in?" Violet asked.

"And why can't we go out and see him?" asked Benny.

"That's just what we were told," said the first guard.

"Yep," said the second guard. "Those are the rules."

"It will be okay, children," said Grandfather Alden. "As I said, I just spoke to Lester on the phone. He says you can come back on the set, so long as you're quiet and well-behaved. You'll be safe there."

"But what about you, Grandfather?" asked Benny. "Where will you be?"

"I'll be here. I'm sure one of these guards will show you back to the studio, won't you?"

"I'm afraid not," said the second guard. "We've got to stay here in case the missing girl turns up."

"That is, if it's a girl that's missing," said the first guard.

"It's okay, Grandfather," Jessie said. "We know our way around the mall. We've been here so many times before."

"And we've already run through it twice today too," said Benny.

"Why don't you children get yourselves something for lunch," Grandfather suggested.

"You must be getting hungry."

"That's the best idea I've heard all day!" said Benny.

"We'll get something to eat soon, Benny. But first let's get back to the studio."

The children told their grandfather good-bye and walked back through the mall.

"This sure seems serious, guys," Violet said. "There are guards and everything."

The Aldens made their way back through the crowd of fans. Violet kept falling behind a few steps because she was having a hard time walking fast in her best shoes, which she had worn just for the show. Once, as she paused to adjust them, Violet thought she saw the man in the dark sunglasses snooping around at the front of the line.

"Look," she said to her siblings. But they were too far ahead to hear her.

Violet shrugged and rushed to catch up with the others. She was more worried about finding Madlynn Rose than paying attention to the mysterious man.

Benny was the first to reach the front of the line and the door to the studio. Knowing that

the sooner they went inside and found Lester, the sooner he would be able to eat, Benny knocked loudly on the door. "Hello!" he called. "It's Benny Alden. Me and my brother and sisters are supposed to come back in!"

Before the other Alden children could hush Benny, the door swung open. There stood Lester, his radio headset still on his head.

"Children, you're back," Lester said, showing the Aldens inside. "I'm very sorry about earlier. I've got a show to run, you see, and time is money. Just stay out of everyone's way, okay?"

"We will," Jessie promised.

But the busy producer had already turned to the production area, where his assistants sat in front of several TV screens playing back the video clips that had been recorded earlier that day.

"There!" Lester yelled, pointing at one of the screens. "See, right there! That's from when Madlynn Rose was here in the studio this morning! Keep that video clip, and find more. This is very important. We need her for the show."

The Alden children caught a glimpse of Madlynn Rose on the screen, sitting behind the judges' table. And then she stood up.

"That moment right there is exactly what we need," said Lester. "That is—children, what did I just tell you about staying out of the way?"

Before the children could see what happened on the screen, Lester shooed them away from the monitors.

"Come on," Henry whispered to his siblings.

"There have to be some clues somewhere," said Jessie.

"Maybe we should see if we can find the other judges," said Violet. "Maybe they have an idea of what's happened to Madlynn Rose."

"That's a great suggestion, Violet," said Henry. "The judges have to be around here somewhere, since nobody's allowed in or out of the mall."

"And we know neither Wilfred Mayflower or Esty Gadooj stepped out *into* the mall," said Jessie, "because all of those fans would have gone crazy."

"You're right," said Henry. "We'd hear them cheering for them."

"Or booing," said Benny. "Booing for that mean Wilfred Mayflower."

As the children walked through the studio, they soon found—and heard—Wilfred Mayflower. The judge was yelling angrily into his cell phone.

"I declare," Wilfred yelled, "I cannot and will not wait around this place all day long just because some girl is missing! You are my manager! You figure out what is wrong and where she's gone. Or else you're *fired*!"

The Aldens tiptoed quietly past the furious judge, not wanting to be yelled at too.

"Well," said Jessie, "we know that Wilfred doesn't know where Madlynn Rose is."

"Or that he had anything to do with her going missing," said Henry. "Let's see what else we can find."

"I hear music," said Benny.

"It sounds great!" said Violet. "It's a band playing an Esty Gadooj song!"

"There's a band on the show?" Henry asked.

"Sure, there is," said Violet. "They play along for all of the singers."

"The music's coming from this way," said Henry. He led his siblings toward the sound.

Behind the big wall with the *Pop Star Sensation* logo, the show's band was playing. There was a guitarist strumming along on a red guitar, a bassist who thumped away on a bass, and a drummer pounding away on a drum set.

In front of the band, dressed in her shiny, puffy, twinkling clothes, was Esty Gadooj, wiggling and shaking and dancing and singing into a microphone. She sang the words to her latest hit song:

> "Get up and shake those hips.
> Get up and move those lips.
> From your toes to your fingertips,
> Get up and dance like this."

All of the Aldens were happy to join in. They liked Esty Gadooj almost as much as Violet liked Madlynn Rose.

"You go, girl!" Esty shouted into her

microphone as Violet spun around. "You're marvelous!"

Henry, Jessie, Violet, and Benny all forgot about the mystery while they joined Esty in twisting and shaking and dancing and twirling.

"You're all really good dancers," Esty said once she had finished her song. "You could all be pop stars someday!"

"Thank you," Violet said bashfully, shy again now that the room was quiet and the attention was all on her and her siblings.

"Thank you, Miss Gadooj," said Jessie, "for letting us dance with you."

"Yeah," said Henry. "Thanks. Can we ask you a question?"

"Why certainly, darlings," Esty said. "You may ask me anything you wish."

"We were in here earlier when they said Madlynn Rose went missing," Henry said, "and now we're trying to figure out where she went."

"Don't worry your pretty little heads, darlings," Esty said. "You're just children. This is a matter for adults to worry about."

"But we want to help," said Jessie. "And we might be young, but..."

"Madlynn Rose is young, just like you," said Esty. "And young people sometimes get into mischief. I'm sure that's all it is, and I'm sure she'll be fine. That's why we're practicing our music. You all just go have fun, and everything will turn out marvelous."

The Alden children walked away from Esty and the *Pop Star Sensation* band.

"We should probably check out the rest of the studio," said Henry.

"But you heard Esty," Jessie said. "She thinks everything will be okay. Maybe she's right."

"But what if everything's not okay?" Violet asked. "What if Madlynn Rose needs our help?"

"Violet's right," Henry said. "We should probably keep searching in case this is a big deal."

"Shh!" Jessie said suddenly. "Listen! This sure sounds like a big deal..."

She nodded toward a dark corner of the studio where someone was talking loudly on a cell phone. The voice was a woman's.

"When word of this gets out," said the woman, "it's going to be everywhere—on the news, all over the Internet, all across social media…"

CHAPTER 5

Lunch and a Hunch

"Madlynn Rose missing will be *huge*."

The children drew closer and saw Madlynn Rose's mother speaking into her cell phone while tapping away at her tablet. But she saw them too and lowered her voice and quickly disappeared down a hallway.

"I wish we could've heard what she was talking about," said Henry. "There might have been a clue to help solve this mystery."

"I know what would help solve the mystery," said Benny. "Lunch!"

"I'm hungry too," said Violet. "I was so nervous earlier that I didn't even eat breakfast."

"That sounds like a good idea," said Jessie. "We could all get something at the food court."

As the Aldens left the studio and walked back into the mall, they ran into Lonny, the girl with the nice voice and the flower in her hair. "Do you know if they're going to let people in to sing soon?" Lonny asked.

"I'm sorry, Lonny," said Henry, "we don't know what's going on."

"They didn't find the missing pop star yet, did they?" Lonny asked. "Do you think they'll just go ahead and do the auditions anyway?"

"I don't think so," said Jessie. "They're all busy trying to figure it out. And now *we're* going to try to figure it out too, over lunch."

"Would you like to come have lunch with us?" Violet asked Lonny.

"I'd better not," said Lonny. "I don't want to lose my place in line. I'm just a regular girl, you know. I don't have the kind of connections you four seem to have, where you can just come and go from a TV studio set."

Violet smiled at Lonny. "We're regular kids too. I guess we're just lucky today, that's all."

The Aldens told Lonny that they'd see her again after lunch and started the long walk through the mall. As they passed the crowds of waiting singers and fans, Violet stopped.

"I thought I saw that man with the sunglasses," she said. "I saw him before too, but we were all running so fast. Why does he keep showing up?"

But there were so many people in line, all of them impatient and loud from the wait, that none of the Aldens could spot the man.

"I'm sure Violet saw him," said Jessie, craning her neck to get a better look.

"It's like he disappeared," said Henry, squinting his eyes.

"We'd better hurry," Benny said, rubbing his belly, "before all the food in the food court disappears too."

At the food court, Jessie gave each of her siblings some money from their grandfather so they could choose what they wanted to eat. "Okay," she said, pointing at an empty table next to the big book store, "we'll all meet here to eat."

Soon the children sat down with their lunches.

Henry took a bite of a fish sandwich. "I think we need to decide who our suspects are so far," he said. "Who would have a reason to want Madlynn Rose to disappear?"

Jessie opened a pack of crackers and crumbled them into the bowl of soup she had bought. She said, "Remember what we just heard Madlynn Rose's mother say? Something about big news? She sure didn't want us to hear any more of what she said. I think she should be a suspect."

"That's a good idea, Jessie," Henry said. "I think another suspect is Lester Freeman."

"But he's Grandfather's friend," said Violet. "He was nice to let us onto the set of *Pop Star Sensation*. And he was going to let me sing. He wouldn't do anything to make Madlynn Rose disappear, would he?"

"I agree that he's nice," said Jessie. "But Henry's right. Remember how he was awfully worried about his show being a 'ratings bonanza'?"

Benny had already eaten his sandwich and was now finishing his lemonade, slurping the cold, sweet liquid quickly through his straw until only the jingly ice was left.

"Benny," said Jessie, "That slurping isn't very polite."

"I'm sorry," said Benny, setting his lemonade cup down and pushing it away to the edge of the table.

"It's okay," said Jessie. "Now, who do you think is a suspect we should investigate?"

"I think that Wilfred Mayflower is pretty mean and grouchy." Benny said.

"But we heard him say that he doesn't know where Madlynn Rose is," said Henry. "And Esty Gadooj doesn't seem very worried at all."

"The other person that I thought wasn't very nice was that lady with the voice that wasn't very good," Benny said.

"That was Super Fan Sophia," said Violet. "She's Madlynn Rose's biggest fan—other than me. She wouldn't do anything bad to her hero, would she?"

"I don't think *anyone* would do anything

bad to her," said Jessie. "But she *is* missing and Sophia sure seemed to think she was a better singer than Madlynn Rose."

"She wasn't even a better singer than Watch!" giggled Benny. "Woof-woof!"

"Sophia also said that a story like this would get millions of people on her website," said Henry. "She *is* the biggest source of Madlynn Rose news on the Internet, she said. I have a hunch maybe she knows more than she told us."

"Well, if you think she's a suspect, then why don't you go ask her," Violet said, pointing into the bookstore. "I see Super Fan Sophia right over there drinking a cup of coffee."

Sure enough, there in the café of the bookstore sat Sophia, sipping a tall and foamy drink and tapping away at her tablet. The Aldens finished their food, threw away their trash, and hurried over to question their super fan suspect. Benny was in such a rush that he knocked his cup of ice off the edge of the table and onto the food court floor.

"Whoops," he said.

"You'd better clean that up," Jessie told him as she headed toward the bookstore.

Benny tried picking up some of the ice but he didn't want to be left behind. He decided he would come back to clean it up later.

Many other fans the children had seen in the line were also packed into the crowded coffee shop and bookstore. The woman with the pink boa was sipping a hot cup of coffee. The cowboy was looking at a magazine about horses. All seven children from the singing family were scattered around the store. The wait seemed to have gotten too long for just about everyone.

The Aldens pressed flat against the café counter and eased their way to where Sophia was sitting, carefully trying not to knock any of the books or other things from the display racks.

"Oops!" said Benny, knocking over some packs of stickers from a rack. He reached down to pick them up. One was a pack of brightly colored flower stickers.

"Those are really pretty," said Jessie.

"Those look familiar," said Henry. "I wish I could remember where I've seen stickers like that before…"

"Look at these stickers," said Benny, picking up another pack that had fallen. "These are letters. They all fell out of the package."

"We should probably buy those," said Jessie, picking the stickers up off the floor. "We shouldn't leave a package that came open because of us."

The Aldens put the flower stickers back on the rack, paid for the alphabet stickers, and walked over to the table where Sophia sat.

"Hello," said Sophia, not looking up from her tablet. "Can't you see that I'm busy?"

"I sure hope you're not telling the whole world about our secret," said Jessie. "You promised that you wouldn't."

"I haven't told anyone yet," said Sophia. "I'm just checking to make sure none of the other Madlynn Rose websites have broken the news. If they do, then *they* will be the ones to get millions of visitors on their sites."

"That's why we wanted to talk to you," said Henry, careful to speak quietly. "Do you know something about Madlynn Rose going missing? Because a story like that would make your website pretty famous, wouldn't it?"

"I would never do anything mean to her," Sophia said. "I'm her biggest fan."

"Besides me," said Violet.

"Besides you," said Sophia. "All I wanted to do was to come here and see her and sing for her."

"Then why did you get out of the line?" Jessie asked. "If you wanted to sing so badly, you wouldn't have left and lost your spot."

"But I didn't lose my spot," Sophia said, sipping her coffee. "That girl with the really nice voice—"

"Lonny," said Henry. "Lonny Dreams, right?"

"Yeah, Lonny," said Sophia. "She said she would save my spot for me. I feel bad for not being very nice to her, because she was *very* nice to me."

"Okay," said Henry, "then maybe you can help us. You know a lot about Madlynn Rose. Who would *you* suspect if you were trying to solve this mystery?"

"I don't know *who* would make her disappear," said Sophia, "but I *do* know that I saw something kind of weird as I walked over here."

"A man with a black suit and sunglasses?" Benny asked.

"No," laughed Sophia, "although I did see a guy like that near where we were standing. What I saw that I thought was strange was Madlynn Rose's mother. I saw her going into the beauty salon."

"I saw that place," said Jessie. "It's between that clothing store and the video game store, right?"

"That's the one," Sophia said. "I just think it's weird for someone whose daughter is missing to be worried about looking good."

"You're right," Jessie said, looking at the other Aldens. "It is weird."

Benny and Violet nodded in agreement.

"Looks like we should head to the salon to talk to our next suspect," Henry said.

CHAPTER 6

Mother Knows Best?

Benny led the way through the mall.

They came to an entrance with a sign that read *Silver City Salon and Spa*. A receptionist at the front of the spa stepped in front of the children with her hand raised and a stern look on her face.

"Kids," she said, "this is not a playground. There is no running allowed in our salon. And children aren't allowed here either unless they are paying customers."

"We're sorry, ma'am," said Henry. "We

just thought someone we wanted to talk to was inside. Is there any way you would let us look around?"

The receptionist pointed at a sign above the cash register. The sign said, *Paying customers only.*

That gave Henry an idea. "Jessie," he said, "do you have any of our lunch money left?"

Jessie reached into her pocket and pulled out what money was left—three one-dollar bills, two quarters, two nickels, and three pennies. She let the money jingle onto the counter and the children counted it up.

"Three dollars and sixty-three cents," said Henry. "Is that enough to buy something in your salon?"

"It certainly won't afford you a mud mask, a facial, or a hairdo," said the receptionist. "But it might buy you one of our less expensive hair accessories." With a wave of her hand, the woman showed the children a wall of hair bands and hair clips and bobby pins and brushes and combs.

"Look at those wigs!" Benny laughed, pointing to the shelves above the hair accessories.

On the shelves high above their heads were wigs of straight hair, curly hair, long hair, and short, bobbed hair. There were colored wigs of black hair and brown hair and blond hair and even pink hair.

"Look at that purple wig," said Violet. "I think it's kind of pretty."

Jessie couldn't keep herself from smiling either. "That bright blond wig looks just like Lester Freeman's hair," she laughed. "It looks like you can buy any type of hairdo you want here."

"Three dollars and change won't buy you any of those wigs," said the receptionist. "They're very expensive, which is why I'm so angry that someone stole one earlier today. How about a hairbrush?"

"We'll take it," said Henry, paying for the brush.

"Would you like it in a bag?" the receptionist asked. But Henry didn't wait for her to hand him the brush or his receipt. Since they were now paying customers, he led his siblings into the salon.

Finding Madlynn Rose's mother wasn't

very hard. The Aldens followed the sound of her voice.

"Be careful with that hangnail!" she yelled. "And watch out for the rough spot on my big toe!"

The missing pop star's mother was seated in a comfortable reclining chair. One salon employee furiously filed away at Mrs. Rose's fingernails. Another worker knelt on the floor of the salon, scrubbing at her feet. It was the first time the children had seen her without a cell phone in one hand and a tablet in the other.

"Hello," said Henry.

"Um, hello," Mrs. Rose said, looking up from the beautician filing her nails. "How can I help you children?"

"We came here to talk to you," said Violet.

"You're the one who's my daughter's fan, aren't you? What is it you'd like to talk about?"

"Well," said Jessie, "What do you know about Madlynn being missing?"

"Hush!" hissed Mrs. Rose. "They don't want us talking about that. And I'll have you know, getting a manicure and pedicure is how I deal with stressful situations."

"But shouldn't you be out looking for your daughter?" Jessie asked. "She's missing after all. She could be anywhere."

"Why do you care?"

"Because we want to solve this mystery," said Benny.

"And I care because Madlynn Rose is my hero," said Violet. "I'd be out searching all over Silver City, except they won't let us out of the mall."

"You don't have to go anywhere," said Mrs. Rose, "because I know for a fact that she's still here in the mall."

"How do you know that?" asked Henry.

"When my daughter went missing, I used a GPS tracking app on my cell phone to locate her phone. The app can't show exactly where it is, but it could tell me her phone is still somewhere in this mall."

"But what if your daughter's hurt?" asked Jessie. "What if she needs you? I know if any of us went missing, Grandfather wouldn't stop looking until he'd found us."

"Madlynn Rose and I got into an argument earlier today," said her mother. "She's young and doesn't like the life of a famous pop star—not all of the time, at least. She threatened not to perform for the show today, though I told her that she had to, that it's her job."

"That's kind of sad," said Violet. "Maybe she just wants to be a young person. Maybe she wants to have friends and have fun and go to school."

"My manicures and pedicures aren't going to pay for themselves, are they?" said Mrs. Rose.

"But we heard you on the phone earlier," said Henry, "saying that your daughter's disappearance would be big news."

"I was talking to my daughter's talent agent," said Mrs. Rose. "I told him what I *really* think is going on." She looked around, then whispered so that only the Aldens could hear.

"I think it's all a stunt by that producer, Lester Freeman."

"You think he's behind it?" Violet asked. "He's so nice."

"He may be nice," said the pop star's mother, "but he's always worried about *Pop*

Star Sensation's ratings. If you're looking to get to the bottom of this, I would suggest you look no further than the producer of her television show."

CHAPTER 7

Video Evidence

On the way back to the TV studio, the Aldens passed the audition line. Lonny Dreams was playing her beautiful song again, and many people gathered around to listen.

"*Everybody telling me what to do…*"

"Hey, gang," said Henry, "maybe we should stop for a moment and figure out what we've learned so far."

"There's a furniture store," said Jessie. "I bet we could find somewhere to sit in there."

"That sounds like a good idea," said Violet. "These shoes are hurting my feet."

The Aldens went into the furniture store and found the softest, most comfortable couch they could. It was shaped like an *L* and had a shiny wooden coffee table in front of it. Henry and Jessie sat on one side of the couch, while Violet and Benny sat on the other. Violet put her sore feet up on the table.

"So far, we know who is *not* behind Madlynn Rose's disappearance," said Henry.

"That's right," said Jessie. "We know it's neither of the judges. It's not Esty Gadooj or Wilfred Mayflower."

"Even though he *is* still mean and scary," said Benny.

"And we know it's not Sophia," said Jessie. "Or Mrs. Rose."

Violet wasn't paying close attention to her siblings. She had taken the alphabet stickers out of the pack that they had bought from the bookstore and was trying to spell her name.

"I can't find a *V*," Violet said. "We must have left some of the letters on the ground in the store. The only other letter I have in

Violet is an *E*. And here's a *D*, an *R*, an *A*, and an *M*." Violet spread the letters she had on the coffee table. "All I can spell with these is *dream*." She noticed she didn't have enough of the right letters to also spell out *Madlynn Rose*, but she did have enough to spell *Lonny*.

Jessie interrupted her thoughts. "Violet, you can play with those after we solve this mystery."

"Yeah," said Henry. "We just have to talk to our last suspect—Lester Freeman!"

Violet nodded and swept the letter stickers back into the package. Then she and the others left the furniture store to return to the *Pop Star Sensation* set.

***

Benny knocked on the door to the audition room once again. The door flew open. This time Mr. Mayflower answered.

"What are you children doing here again?" asked Wilfred Mayflower. "I hope you're here to tell me that silly pop star has been found and that we can get on with the show."

"We're sorry, Mr. Mayflower," said Violet, closing the door once she and her siblings were inside the studio. "We're still trying to find her."

"I didn't expect *you* to have found her," Wilfred said.

"But we're really good at solving mysteries," Benny said.

"I highly doubt that," said Wilfred. "Children are *horrible* at most everything, except for making a lot of racket and making me angry."

"But you're always angry," said Benny.

Wilfred didn't have a reply for that.

"Like my brother, Benny, said, we're trying to help," said Henry. "We need to talk with Lester Freeman. We need to ask him some questions."

"I'd like to ask Lester some questions too," Wilfred said, "but I don't know where he or his camera crew have run off to."

Wilfred Mayflower stomped off in a huff, leaving the children alone in the studio surrounded by the judges' table, the many TV screens, and the *Pop Star Sensation* sign.

"We've got to find Mr. Freeman," Violet said. "We have to ask if he knows anything about Madlynn Rose's disappearance."

From behind the table and big sign came a few musical sounds. The Alden children followed them.

The *Pop Star Sensation* band sat fiddling with their instruments. The bass player tuned the strings of his bass. The drummer impatiently tapped the pedal of his bass drum. The guitarist strummed his bright red guitar, playing the chords for Madlynn Rose's hit song. Violet couldn't help but stop and sing along.

> "It feels like time to say hello,
> But, sorry, now I've got to go.
> One last thing you've got to know,
> This won't be good-bye, oh no.
> This won't be good-bye.
> This won't be good-bye."

Next to the band sat Esty Gadooj. The lights of her costume weren't flashing anymore and now she looked bored.

"Miss Gadooj!" said Jessie. "We need your help. Do you know where Mr. Freeman is? We've got to ask him about Madlynn Rose."

"He's out with the film crew," Esty Gadooj replied. "They're in the mall somewhere. I told them it was no use."

Suddenly there was a clatter and a crash. Benny hadn't been looking where he was going and had fallen into an open and empty guitar case.

"Oops!" Benny said, climbing out of the case. "I accidentally bumped into that rack of guitars, and I fell. I'm okay though."

"Let's make sure all of these guitars are okay," said Jessie. She walked over to the guitar rack, where several guitars were swinging after being bumped by the youngest Alden.

Jessie looked the guitars over to make sure they hadn't been chipped or scratched. There were six spaces on the guitar rack, but only four guitars. She couldn't help but notice that the four were orange, yellow, green, and blue. She turned and saw the band's guitarist with a red guitar.

"Those guitar colors make a rainbow," she said, pointing from the red guitar to the others. "Well, almost. There's not a purple guitar."

Henry pointed to the empty space at the end of the rack. "But if there was a purple guitar, it could go right there. Then you'd have your rainbow, Jessie."

"I guess I would," said Jessie. "It's a good thing Benny didn't damage any of them. It would have cost a lot to have them repaired." She turned to the band members and apologized for the trouble.

"And we're sorry for bothering you, Miss Gadooj," said Violet.

"And all of you musicians too," said Henry.

No closer to solving the mystery of the missing pop star, the Alden children sadly shuffled back to the TV show set. There, something on one of TV screens made Benny Alden very excited.

"There I am!" shouted Benny. "On the big TV!"

"It's this morning's taping," said Jessie.

"If they recorded us," said Henry, "then maybe they recorded what happened here in the studio before we got here."

"Maybe they recorded what happened to Madlynn Rose!" said Violet.

"Excuse me, sir," said Jessie to one of the *Pop Star Sensation* crew members sitting in front of the TV screen, "can you rewind the recording to the beginning?"

The man at the controls shrugged. "Sure. It's easy. You kids can even work the keyboard yourself, if you'd like."

"I'd love to," said Henry.

In a second, the Aldens were watching the *Pop Star Sensation* set as it had looked at the very start of the day.

On the screen, all three judges sat at their table—grumpy Wilfred Mayflower, flashy Esty Gadooj, and the not-yet-missing Madlynn Rose.

In the video, Madlynn Rose whispered something that the children couldn't hear into Esty Gadooj's ear. Then Madlynn Rose got up from her seat and walked to a side door of the studio. Without looking back, she walked out and the door closed behind her.

"Wait!" Violet said. "Henry, could you go back a bit? I think I saw something."

Henry rewound the film.

"Pause it," said Violet. "Right there."

There, on the screen, in the doorway that Madlynn Rose had just walked out of, was the figure of a very creepy-looking man wearing dark sunglasses and a dark suit.

"Come on," said Violet. "We've got to find him."

CHAPTER 8

The Strange Man

The Aldens hurried out into the Silver City Mall. Henry led the way.

"Hey!" a voice shouted from the audition line. It was Lonny.

"Lonny," said Henry, already out of breath, "have you seen a strange man?"

"I've seen lots of strange men today in this audition line," Lonny laughed. "I've seen silly-looking old ladies and men dressed like cowboys. Why, I even saw a whole group of kids in matching outfits."

"Well," said Henry, "we're looking for a guy with—"

"There he is!" Benny shouted, spotting the strange man in the dark sunglasses not far from where he and his siblings stood.

But the man realized he'd been seen. He began to run in the other direction, and the children chased after him. The man was faster though, and he weaved through the mall crowds until the Aldens lost sight of him. The children slowed to a stop.

"We lost him," Henry sighed.

"Wait, where's Violet?" Jessie asked, looking around for her sister.

"I think her shoes were slowing her down," said Benny.

"The other question is, where is the strange man?" Henry asked.

The three Alden children waited for their sister to catch up. While they waited, they looked around, scanning the crowd and the entrances to the many busy shops.

"He's not over that way," said Benny, pointing toward the video game store.

"All I see there are mannequins with

colorful blue jeans and jackets," said Jessie, pointing to one of the clothing stores.

"All I see there is a mannequin with a dark suit and dark sun—it's him!" shouted Henry.

The mysterious man had hidden himself in the display of one of the clothing stores. Next to a mannequin wearing a beautiful evening dress and another wearing a fancy leather jacket, the man they were chasing was trying to stand perfectly still. But once he saw that the Alden children had spotted him, the man leaped from the display and again began to run.

As the man ran, he dodged people left and right, sometimes bumping into them. He knocked the shopping bags out of a woman's hands. He nearly collided with a café table. He narrowly avoided getting tangled up in a long line of children.

Jessie stopped to help the woman with the shopping bags while Henry and Benny dashed through the crowd after the man. The man reached the food court and ran past the table where the Aldens had eaten their lunch only a short while earlier.

Benny saw the cup of ice he'd spilled still lying on the floor. And then he saw the man's feet hit the patch of icy, slippery water.

"Aaaah!" the man shouted as he slipped and fell flat onto the floor of the Silver City Mall.

"We've got you!" Benny Alden shouted as he and Henry and Jessie finally caught up to the strange man who now lay on his back, staring up at the mall ceiling.

"Who are you?" Henry asked the man.

"And do you know about Madlynn Rose?" added Jessie.

"Okay, okay," said the man, "you've got me. I'll answer your questions. Just help me up first."

Henry reached down and helped the man up. Jessie pulled out one of the chairs from the table where the children had eaten their lunch and let the man sit.

"Thank you," the man said. "I thought I could outrun you since it's my job to be fast and strong. I guess I couldn't. Or I couldn't outrun that slippery puddle."

"I'm sorry," said Benny. "That was my mess."

"And this is *my* mess," said the man. "You see, I'm a bodyguard."

"What's that?" asked Benny.

"I watch over famous people," the man explained. "I protect them and make sure they stay safe."

"That sounds like fun," said Benny. "Kind of like being a policeman, huh?"

"Kind of," the man laughed. "Well, I'm the bodyguard for one famous person in particular."

"Who?" Benny asked.

"I can't say," said the man.

"You said you would answer our questions," said Jessie.

"Fine," said the man. "I'm the bodyguard for the famous pop star, Madlynn Rose."

"If you're her bodyguard, then what happened to her?" Jessie asked. "She's missing, so you must not have done your job very well."

"Did you make her disappear?" asked Benny.

"I guess you could say that," said the man. "Or I *let* her disappear anyway. Although I know where she's been the whole time."

"Do you know where she is now?" asked Henry.

"I know where she was when I left her," said the man. "But I can't tell you where that is."

"Why not?" asked Jessie.

"Because it's a secret," the bodyguard said. "I promised I wouldn't tell."

"Hold on, guys," called Violet, walking across the food court toward them.

"Violet!" Jessie exclaimed. "Where have you been?"

"And who are all those people?" Benny asked.

Violet had a line of people following close behind her, including a man with a shirt that said *Sunglasses Galore*, Lester Freeman and his camera crew carrying clipboards and cameras, Madlynn Rose's mother carefully walking along with her freshly painted toenails. The receptionist from the Silver City Salon and Spa and Super Fan Sophia followed Mrs. Rose. Behind them marched Esty Gadooj and the *Pop Star Sensation* band, all followed by a sweating, huffing, and puffing Wilfred Mayflower.

"I know where Madlynn Rose is," said Violet.

CHAPTER 9

A Ratings Bonanza

"Where is she?" Benny asked.

"How did you find her?" Henry asked.

"Where did you go?" Jessie asked. "We thought you had fallen behind."

"I did fall behind," Violet said. In one hand she held her pair of fancy dress shoes. "My shoes were hurting my feet and I couldn't keep up with you when you ran after the man in the sunglasses."

"This man's job is to guard Madlynn Rose," said Benny. "But he's not very good at his job, because Madlynn Rose is still missing."

"No, she's not," said Violet. "But I'll get to that part in a second. Look what I've got here."

She held up the two items in her other hand: a pair of flower-shaped sunglasses and a wig.

"All day long, we've seen clues," Violet said. "I heard someone sing with a really pretty voice that sounded a little familiar...Then I found these sunglasses..."

"Are you going to pay for those glasses?" asked the man wearing the glasses store shirt. "Or do you plan on returning them?"

"Here, you can have them back," said Violet. "Then I passed the salon. There on the shelf I saw this"—Violet held up a wig of long blond hair.

"You better return that," said the receptionist, "because I know you don't have the money to pay for it."

Violet handed the wig to the woman from the salon.

From the back of the audition line, the Aldens noticed a friendly face nodding to them—as if to say that it was okay to reveal her secret.

"Lonny Dreams—or Madlynn Rose," said Violet, "will you come out and join us?"

Out from the crowd stepped the girl wearing sunglasses and a blond wig and carrying the guitar case covered with stickers.

"Lonny Dreams," said Henry looking at the name on the guitar case. "I get it now. L-O-N-N-Y D-R-E-A-M-S. It's an anagram for M-A-D-L-Y-N-N R-O-S-E."

"And those stickers on your guitar case," pointed Benny, "those are from the bookstore."

"You're right," the girl said, opening the guitar case and taking out the purple guitar from inside it.

"The purple guitar!" said Jessie. "That's the one that was missing from the last spot on the guitar rack. The guitarist had the red one from the first empty spot. Then there were orange, yellow, green, and blue guitars. Like the colors of the rainbow. The last one is this purple one!"

"Yes," the girl said, handing the purple guitar to the guitarist of the *Pop Star Sensation* band.

Then the girl took the flower-shaped sunglasses she was wearing off of her face, and the long, blond wig she was wearing off her head. And the girl who everyone had thought was a singer named Lonny Dreams—

everyone except for Violet Alden—turned back into the pop star named Madlynn Rose.

A crowd had gathered around, and when they recognized Madlynn, they all cheered.

"This is great footage!" shouted Lester, directing his cameramen to film what was happening.

"I can't believe I'm getting this for my website!" said Super Fan Sophia, holding up her tablet and recording the scene.

While the producer and the camera crew and Sophia were all smiles, someone still did not look very happy.

"Honey," said Madlynn Rose's mother, stepping up to the front, "why would you pull such a stunt?"

"I'm tired of being a pop star," said Madlynn Rose.

"But why?" Violet asked. "You're famous and everyone loves you."

"That's the trouble," said Madlynn Rose. "I can't go anywhere without everyone noticing me." The pop star pointed at the crowd who now surrounded her.

"And when you're a pop star," she continued,

"how do you know if people are cheering for your talent, or if they're just cheering for you because you're famous?"

"You have talent," said Wilfred Mayflower. "You might not have a good sense of knowing when not to worry all of us, but you are definitely *not* a terrible singer."

"I understand what she is trying to say, darling," said Esty Gadooj. "As a pop star myself, sometimes all of the hubbub stops being fabulous and starts to be frustrating. Which is why when Madlynn Rose whispered her plan to me..."

"So *that's* what you two were whispering about on the video," said Henry.

"When I whispered my plan to Esty," Madlynn Rose said, "she told me it was a marvelous idea. So I did it. I wanted to see if people would like me for who I am. I'm sorry that I caused all this trouble."

"It's no trouble for me," said Lester, his cameras catching every word. "This will be a ratings bonanza!"

CHAPTER 10

The Purple Guitar

The two security guards from the front entrance of the Silver City Mall along with James Alden appeared at the door to the *Pop Star Sensation* studio.

"I guess the secret's not a secret anymore," said the first guard.

"And I guess the mystery's been solved," said the second guard, "thanks to your grandkids."

Grandfather was smiling proudly. He walked into the studio and was greeted by the warm hugs of his four grandchildren.

"I can't wait to tell you about our day!" said Henry.

"We missed you, Grandfather!" said Jessie.

"I got to meet Madlynn Rose!" said Violet.

"And my lemonade spilled!" said Benny.

"I'm glad to see you," Grandfather Alden said.

Then they all sat back and watched while Lester directed the cameras toward the judges' table, where Wilfred, Esty, and Madlynn sat.

Wilfred Mayflower looked slightly less grumpy than usual. "I'm sorry for many of the unfriendly things I've said in the past, Madlynn Rose," Wilfred told the youngest judge. "My behavior was *horrible*, and I will try harder from now on to judge people fairly. You, my dear, have a wonderful voice, no matter who you are. Please stay here at this judging table, I beg you."

The flashing lights were blinking all over Esty Gadooj's costume again. "My darling young lady," she said to Madlynn Rose, "while I wasn't worried about where you were, I *was* worried that you weren't feeling marvelous.

Please know that not only do I think you're marvelous—but the whole world does too. Okay, darling?"

Madlynn Rose smiled and thanked her two friends. Then she called out to someone in the audience.

"Mom," said Madlynn Rose, "I'd like to apologize for going missing and worrying you. I thought the only thing you cared about was my career and my fame. But I realize that you care about me. I don't need to dress up as someone else or be anything other than your girl. And instead of worrying about my career, all I want you to do is be my mom. I might be famous, but I'm still your little girl. I'm still me."

Then Madlynn Rose pointed to someone else seated behind the cameras, motioning for that person to step forward.

"Super Fan Sophia, please come up here," said the pop star. "I'd like to thank you for all the hard work you've done, telling my fans about me and my music. I'd like to announce that your website will now be the official spot where my fans can hear my latest songs and read about my latest tours and all my latest news. Super Fan Sophia, you're now officially my online Super-est Super Fan, and your website is now my official Internet home."

Sophia didn't seem to know what to say. Tears streamed down her face and she had to put down her tablet to wipe them away and give her favorite pop star a great big hug.

"I'd like to introduce some other folks," Madlynn Rose continued. She waved her hand to the show's technical crew, and with a flick of a switch, the wall behind the judges' table rose out of the way. For the first time in front of the cameras, stood the band behind Madlynn Rose's music. The drummer tapped his sticks, the bassist thumped his bass, and the guitarist strummed some chords on his red guitar. Then he stopped and picked up the purple guitar. He handed it to Madlynn Rose and the two of them began to play.

"In just a moment, we're going to start the show and let these wonderful people in to audition for *Pop Star Sensation*," said Madlynn

Rose. "But before we do that, I'd like to sing a new song."

The chords and notes of the song sounded familiar to Violet. It was a song she'd heard earlier that day. And then she heard her own name being spoken...by Madlynn Rose!

"Violet Alden, I'd like you to come up here and help me sing this song. I hear you're pretty great at solving mysteries and finding missing people, but that you're even better at singing!"

Violet jumped out of her seat and ran up to join Madlynn Rose and the band. She happily sang the words she'd learned earlier that day, singing them with the pop star whom she'd found:

> "Everybody telling me what to do,
> Everyone telling me who I should be,
> But I can't be you or you or you.
> I'll follow my dreams and be me.
> So let me be me.
> Please let me be me."

When Madlynn and Violet finished singing

the song, the entire audience cheered, along with millions of people watching at home. But nobody was prouder than Henry, Jessie, Benny, and Grandfather, who were happy that Violet was Violet.

THE BOXCAR CHILDREN Fan Club

Join the Boxcar Fan Club!

Visit **boxcarchildren.com** and receive a free goodie
bag when you sign up. You'll receive occasional
newsletters and be eligible to win prizes
and more! Sign up today!

Don't Forget!

The Boxcar Children audiobooks are also available!
Find them at your local bookstore, or visit
oasisaudio.com for more information.

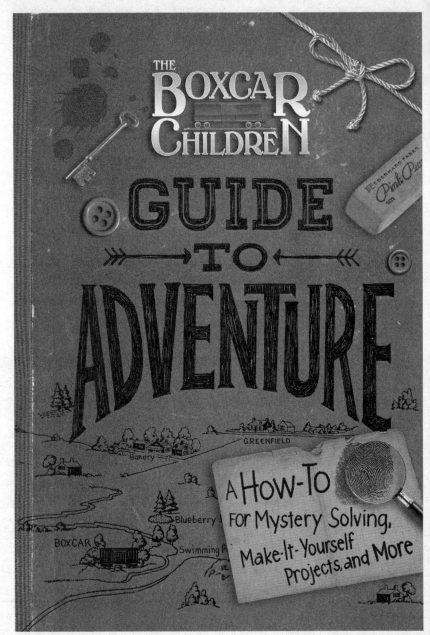

THE BOXCAR CHILDREN

GUIDE
→→→ TO ←←←
ADVENTURE

GREENFIELD

Bakery

Blueberry

BOXCAR

Swimming P

A HOW-TO
For Mystery Solving,
Make-It-Yourself
Projects, and More

ISBN: 9780807509050, $12.99

Discover how the Boxcar Children's adventures began!

THE
BOXCAR
CHILDREN®
BEGINNING

"Fans will enjoy this picture of life 'before.'"
—*Publishers Weekly*

Before they were the Boxcar Children, Henry, Jessie, Violet, and Benny Alden lived with their parents on Fair Meadow Farm.

NEWBERY MEDAL-WINNER
PATRICIA MACLACHLAN

PB ISBN: 9780807566176, $5.99

The adventures continue in the newest mysteries!

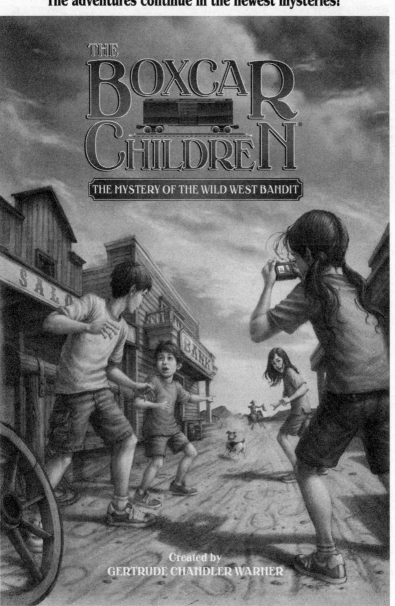

THE BOXCAR CHILDREN

THE MYSTERY OF THE GRINNING GARGOYLE

Created by
GERTRUDE CHANDLER WARNER

PB ISBN: 9780807508930, $5.99

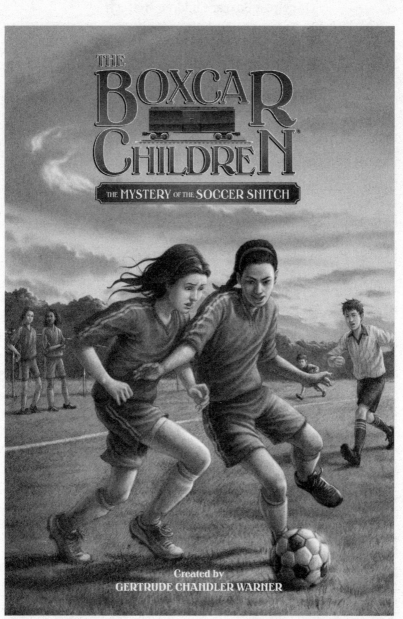

THE BOXCAR CHILDREN®

THE MYSTERY OF THE SOCCER SNITCH

Created by
GERTRUDE CHANDLER WARNER

PB ISBN: 9780807508961, $5.99

THE
BOXCAR
CHILDREN

THE MYSTERY OF THE
STOLEN DINOSAUR BONES

Created by
GERTRUDE CHANDLER WARNER

PB ISBN: 9780807556085, $5.99

Watch followed the children into the cave. "Do you smell any clues, Watch?" Jessie asked. Watch sniffed around the floor. He stopped near the ladder marks and looked up and wagged his tail.

"I think Watch wants us to go up into that passageway too," said Violet.

"He sniffs something," said Jessie.

"Let's check it out," said Henry. "I'll go first."

Henry and Jessie set their ladder against

the cave wall. Henry climbed up while Jessie held the ladder steady. He shined his headlight into the passageway before crawling in.

"Be careful," called Violet. She looked around nervously. The shadows from their flashlights made the cave walls look like they were alive.

"I think I hear something," whispered Benny. He shined his flashlight on a dark corner. Something scurried out of the light beam.

"What is it?" cried Violet.

Jessie slowly walked over and shined her light around the cave floor. She gasped as a dark brown mouse scampered between her feet and zipped across the floor. It disappeared inside a crack in the wall.

"What else lives inside this cave?" asked Violet. She shivered.

"Henry," Jessie called. "Watch out for cave creatures up there!"

Just then Henry poked his head out of the passageway. "Come on up!" he said. "Just watch your step."

Jessie helped Benny and Violet up. Then Jessie handed up Watch and crawled in after him. There was room for everyone to crouch. The passageway headed into the darkness.

"We just have to crawl for a few feet, then the passageway gets taller and wider," said Henry. "It's very dark and some places are muddy."

"We'll be very careful," said Jessie. "And stick together. Right, everyone?"

The children agreed. They crawled slowly through the rocky passageway. The bright lights on their caving helmets and their flashlights showed the way. Soon the passageway became large enough for the children to stand up.

"Look over there," said Violet. She pointed to an opening. The children saw a small cavern just below them. "Should we go in there?"

"I think so," said Jessie. "We'll all go together and keep close."

They carefully stepped into the cavern and shined their flashlights around the floor.

"Oh, I see some tracks," said Violet. "They're in the mud by that opening in the wall."

Jessie tiptoed over and shined her light on the cave floor. She drew in her breath and looked back at her siblings.

"What's wrong?" asked Henry. "Are they footprints?" They joined Jessie by the muddy tracks.

"Oh, those aren't footprints," said Violet.

"Not from a person," said Jessie. "They look like bird tracks..."

"Very big bird tracks!" said Violet. "They're huge! What kind of bird makes tracks that big?" She looked around and hugged herself.

"I know!" cried Benny. "It's a real, live dinosaur!"

Just then Watch started barking.

GERTRUDE CHANDLER WARNER discovered when she was teaching that many readers who like an exciting story could find no books that were both easy and fun to read. She decided to try to meet this need, and her first book, *The Boxcar Children*, quickly proved she had succeeded.

Miss Warner drew on her own experiences to write the mystery. As a child she spent hours watching trains go by on the tracks opposite her family home. She often dreamed about what it would be like to set up housekeeping in a caboose or freight car—the situation the Alden children find themselves in.

While the mystery element is central to each of Miss Warner's books, she never thought of them as strictly juvenile mysteries. She liked to stress the Aldens' independence and resourcefulness and their solid New England devotion to using up and making do. The Aldens go about most of their adventures with as little adult supervision as possible—something else that delights young readers.

Miss Warner lived in Putnam, Connecticut, until her death in 1979. During her lifetime, she received hundreds of letters from girls and boys telling her how much they liked her books.